To Adam
S. MᶜB.

To Eden, with love
I. B.

ISBN 0-439-07773-7

Text copyright © 1998 by Sam McBratney.
Illustrations copyright © 1998 by Ivan Bates.
All rights reserved. Published by Scholastic Inc.,
555 Broadway, New York, NY 10012, by arrangement
with Candlewick Press. SCHOLASTIC and
associated logos are trademarks and/or registered
trademarks of Scholastic Inc.

12 11 10 9 8 7 6 5 4 3 2 1   8 9/9 0 1 2 3/0

Printed in the U.S.A.   14

First Scholastic printing, September 1998

This book was typeset in Golden Type.
The pictures were done in watercolor and
colored pencil.

Sam McBratney

Just You and Me

illustrated by Ivan Bates

SCHOLASTIC INC.
New York Toronto London Auckland Sydney
Mexico City New Delhi Hong Kong

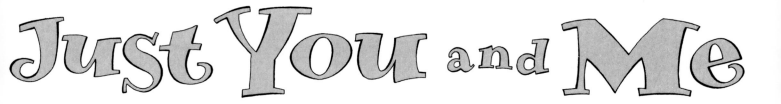

Once there was a little gosling goose and her name was **Little Goosey.**

One day **Little Goosey** and **Big Gander Goose,** who looked after her, set out to walk down to the river.

They hadn't gone far when the wind began to blow.
Gander Goose looked up at the dark clouds racing
across the sky and said, "A storm is coming.

We'd better find a place to hide."
"A nice warm place? Just for me
and you?" said Little Goosey.
"Just us," said Gander Goose.
"A place where we can rest
until the storm is over."
And they hurried into the
woods, looking for a place to hide.
"Will there be thunder when the
storm comes?"asked Little Goosey.
"Well, yes, there could be some thunder,"
said Gander Goose.

Soon they found a hole in a ditch, but there was
someone in there already—a small gray-whiskered
mouse. She was hiding from the storm, too.
"You can stay in here with me if you like,"
said the mouse.

Little Goosey whispered
to Gander Goose,
"I don't want anybody else
when the thunder comes.

Just me and you."

Gander Goose thanked the small gray-whiskered mouse. "It's a bit too damp in here for us," he said. "You're very kind, but I think we'll look for someplace else. Good-bye."

When the other two had gone, the mouse saw some wet moss growing up the walls. "It *is* a bit damp in here," she thought to herself. "I'll look for a better place, too."

Little **G**oosey and **G**ander **G**oose went farther
into the woods, looking for a place to hide. They
found a hole among the roots of a tall tree,
but there was someone in there already—
a squirrel with a high, proud tail.
"Would you like to stay in here with me?"
said the squirrel.

Little Goosey whispered to
Gander Goose,
"But I don't want anybody else.

Just me and you."

Gander Goose thanked the squirrel with the high, proud tail. "I can see daylight above our heads," he said. "You're very kind, but I think we'll look for someplace else. Good-bye."

When the other two had gone, the squirrel looked up and saw the sky through the trunk of the hollow tree. "The rain *could* easily run in through that hole," he thought to himself. "I'll try to find a better place, too."

Little **G**oosey and **G**ander **G**oose ventured
farther into the woods. They found an interesting
cave among the rocks, but a rabbit with
furry ears had found it before them.
"We could all stay here together if you like,"
said the rabbit.

Little Goosey nestled into the
soft feathers of Gander Goose, and said quietly,
"I don't want there to be anybody else
when the thunder comes.

Just me and you."

Gander Goose thanked the rabbit with furry ears.
"There are too many stones in here for us," he said.
"You're very kind, but I think we'll look for
someplace else. Good-bye."

When the other two had gone, the rabbit couldn't
find a space to lie down comfortably.
"It *is* too stony in here," she thought to herself.
"I'll look for a better place, too."

Little Goosey was beginning to feel tired after
all that searching for a place to hide, but then they
found a hole behind a bush at the bottom of a hill.
"This looks like a good place to be out of the storm,"
said Gander Goose. "And there's no one here."

"Just us," yawned Little Goosey.
She made a tunnel under some blown-in leaves
so that she wouldn't hear the thunder if it came,
and she lay down to sleep.

The storm arrived.
A great wind blew through the
trees and the rain came down.
In the fields and in the woods no one
could be seen, for they were all
hiding from the storm.

The dark clouds passed over. The wind died
down and soon the skies were clear again.
Little **G**oosey blinked in the ray of
sunlight shining into the hole.
Then she heard someone behind her.

"This was a good place to hide from the storm,"
said the small gray-whiskered mouse.
"It was," agreed the squirrel with the high, proud tail.
"A very good place to hide from the storm,"
said the rabbit with furry ears.

The mouse, the squirrel, and the rabbit waved
good-bye and then ran off into the woods.
"This was a good place to hide from the storm."
Little Goosey laughed. "For all of us!"

Gander Goose looked out at the trees, still
dripping after all the rain. "It was. And now
I think we'll walk down to the river," he said.

"Just us?"
asked **L**ittle **G**oosey.
Gander **G**oose
smiled and said,

"Just you and me."